Magic Mansion

Sara Grant

Illustrated by Erica-Jane Waters

Orion
Children's Books

First published in Great Britain in 2014
by Orion Children's Books
a division of the Orion Publishing Group Ltd
Orion House
5 Upper St Martin's Lane
London WC2H 9EA
An Hachette UK company

1 3 5 7 9 10 8 6 4 2

The Orion Publishing Group's policy is to use papers
that are natural, renewable and recyclable products and
made from wood grown in sustainable forests. The logging
and manufacturing processes are expected to conform to the
environmental regulations of the country of origin.

A catalogue record for this book is
available from the British Library.

ISBN 978 1 4440 0787 9

Printed in Great Britain by Clays Ltd, St Ives plc

To my lovely agent Jenny Savill –
the fairy godmother who made
my wishes come true!

Magic Mansion

Collect all the Magic Trix *books*

- ❏ The Witching Hour
- ❏ Flying High
- ❏ Birthday Wishes
- ❏ Museum Mayhem
- ❏ Secrets and Spies
- ☑ Magic Mansion

Chapter One

Creeping cats! Trix's world had been turned upside down. Really and truly!

She was dangling like a bat from the chandelier in Magic Mansion's grand ballroom. All the witches in the Sisterhood of Magic were gathered below. Their eyes and tiaras twinkled up at her. The chandelier's crystals jingled and jangled like chimes in a hurricane as she swung back and forth in time

to the orchestra's music – and the gasps of the crowd.

She bent her knees to grip the chandelier, but she could feel herself slipping. What had started as an enchanted adventure was ending as a nightmare.

Her beautiful yellow ballgown, which had once shimmered like the summer sun, was in tatters. She was missing one of her shoes and Jinx, her magical familiar, was hanging by a paw from the hem of her gown.

Tonight should have been the most magical night of her life, but it had gone terribly wrong. Trix loved being a witch. She had tried her best to learn everything her magical tutor, Lulu, had taught her. She had practised her spells and flying and potions like a good witch-in-training but, no matter how hard she tried, she seemed to be the very best at making magical messes. And *this* was the most spectacular super-duper mess of them all.

Meow! Jinx cried, his claw etching tracks in the silky fabric as he inched lower and lower.

"Hold on, Jinx," Trix called, catching the black and white kitten as the last threads of her hem gave way.

She held Jinx close and felt the thrum of his purrs. "How are we ever going to get out of this mess?" she whispered.

A smile tugged at the edges of Trix's lips. She had to admit that she must look silly up here. She liked hanging upside down on the climbing frame at school – the way it made her tummy flutter and her head feel fuzzy.

This might even have been fun – if everyone from the Sisterhood of Magic wasn't staring at her in shock and horror, *and* if she couldn't see Stella smugly smirking, *and* if Trix didn't feel her grip on the chandelier loosening.

She had almost forgotten she was a witch. All she needed was the right spell to keep her from falling, repair her dress and erase everyone's memory of this oh-so-embarrassing moment, but that type of magic was very big for a little witch-in-training.

She couldn't let go of Jinx, and her brain couldn't think of a word that rhymed with upside down or right-side up!

Creeping cats!

How had tonight gone so topsy-turvy? It had started so wonderfully, with an unexpected invitation.

Chapter Two

Earlier that night . . .

Trix was snuggled in her bed, but she couldn't sleep. It was as if a hundred million films were playing at the same time in her head. Her body buzzed like it did after a birthday party when fizzy drink mixed with chocolate cake and sweets and presents and surprises and friends and . . . *Whoa!*

Trix took a deep breath. The tail of her black cat clock swished from side to side with each tick-tock. It was nearly ten o'clock. She could hear her little brother, Oscar, snoring and her parents climbing the stairs to bed. Her head knew it was time to sleep, but her body didn't feel like it. She looked around for Jinx. Where had that crazy cat gone? He loved to play games – especially at bedtime when everyone else in the Morgan family was sleeping. She sat bolt upright in her bed, sending the twenty-three cat toys she slept with flying into the air.

"Jinx," Trix whispered and checked under her bed. "Jinx?" She peeked in her wardrobe. He wasn't hiding among her clothes and mismatched shoes and socks. Her curtains swished and light streamed in around the edges. "Jinx?" She drew back the curtains, expecting to see the sparkling spots of her black and white kitten, but instead all she saw was the big, bright full moon.

She sighed. Her Aunt Belle was right – full moons were magical. She remembered the first magical moment she'd ever had. At midnight on her tenth birthday, she'd spotted Lulu riding on her broom across the moon. Only witches could see another witch's midnight ride. Trix could hardly believe her eyes that night and, the next day, Lulu had had to convince Trix she really was a witch! There were times, like this one, when she still wondered if it were true or just a dream.

A spark of light on the big bright moon seemed to blink. She rubbed her eyes. Maybe she was sleepy after all. The dot of light grew bigger and bigger. It darted back and forth through the night sky. Was it a bird or a bat?

It zigzagged in a crazy pattern and was now heading straight for Trix. She thought she could hear the sound of crinkling paper, or was it the flapping of wings? She ducked as a shimmering envelope shot through the open window and landed with a *whoosh* right in the middle of her bed. Her name was written on the front in glittering pink.

How exciting! A magical message just for Trix! She ripped open the envelope. Inside was a single sheet of stationery. At first glance, the paper looked blank, but when she moved it into a beam of moonlight, curlicues of writing appeared on the page.

It was an advanced magic spell – with instructions to recite the spell as the clock struck ten. Trix glanced at her cat clock. Ten o'clock was only minutes away!

Trix remembered the special advanced magic Lulu had used for their magical midnight ride to London. It had allowed them to be gone for the night without anyone missing them. Oh, how she loved the possibilities of magic! And she hoped this was the start of another night-time adventure.

But where was Jinx? Trix searched her

room again. Jinx would definitely want to come along.

"Jinx," she whispered, checking every possible hiding spot, but he was nowhere to be found. Trix shuffled her feet into her slippers and strapped on her big green watch.

Meow! Meow!

She jumped at the sound, but it wasn't her magical familiar. It was her black cat clock striking ten o'clock. There was no time to lose. She and Jinx had a magical connection. He would find her wherever she went. Trix read the spell. A cool breeze whipped through her hair and ruffled the hundreds of cats printed on her pyjamas so they looked as if they were racing round and round her body. Then she felt the tingly rush of magical transportation.

Chapter Three

Jinx scampered around the magic classroom, hippity-hopping here and there and everywhere. He was so excited that he couldn't sit still. He leaped from the bookcase full of Lulu's weird and wonderful ingredients to the wardrobe stuffed with magnificently magical bits and bobs. His magical familiar friends were there too. Tabby the cat chased after Jinx, the end of her tail flicking nervously. Rascal, a rambunctious pug, snuffled along the edge

of the classroom as if sniffing out clues. Twitch, the
lavender rat, was perched on the lip of the cauldron.
Sherlock the owl flapped about hooting, as if he
were asking a question: "Who? Who? Who?"

Lulu had summoned the familiars to the magic
classroom and told them a secret. Oooooh, it was
such a super-big gigantic secret. And then she had
disappeared. Secrets made Jinx's whiskers itch and
his tail twitch. Lulu had made them promise they
wouldn't tell their witches. It was a surprise – the
best surprise any witch-in-training could ever
receive in the whole universe. None of the witches-
in-training knew it yet, but tonight was the annual
Sisterhood of Magic Ball! Jinx loved parties, and this

was the most spectacular and magical of them all.

But the time for celebration would come later. Now was the time for fun and games. Each new witch would have to pass a few tests before she could go to the party. The ball was at Magic Mansion, which was the top-secret headquarters of the Sisterhood of Magic. None of the witches-in-training were supposed to know that, but Jinx had taken Trix there once to cheer her up.

From the outside, Magic Mansion looked like an old ramshackle house that might topple over if a cat sneezed in its direction, but inside it was the most glamorous and glorious place you could ever imagine.

Trix would be here any minute. Jinx hated waiting; it was worse than having a hungry, rumbly tummy because no snack could satisfy the buzzy-bee feeling of waiting. Oh, how he wanted Trix to arrive, right now. Now. NOW!

Jinx's nose began to itch. His whiskers started to twitch. He planted himself in the middle of the magic classroom. The tip of his tail flicked left, then right, and he blinked his big golden eyes as a Trix shape appeared in a glimmer of light.

Meow! Meow! Jinx greeted his witch.

Trix rubbed her eyes as her witch's hat magically appeared on top of her head. Her pyjamas were wrinkled and her slippers didn't match – one was pink and the other green. Her curls jetted out in every direction as if they were  autumn leaves being blown in the wind, but that was what Jinx liked about Trix. She was original.

"I've been looking all over for you, Jinx!" Trix placed a kiss on his furry head. Jinx's spots sparkled. That's what they always did when he was happy. He couldn't wait for their magical adventure to begin!

Rascal barked when his witch arrived. He raced circles around Stella. If she hadn't been wearing her perfectly pink pyjamas, Jinx never would have guessed it was past her bedtime. Her hair was smooth and straight, and peeking from under her pyjama bottoms was a pair of bright white trainers.

"What are YOU doing here?" Stella moaned when she saw Trix. Stella was like those sweets that look lovely on the outside but taste sour on the inside. Jinx's lips puckered at the thought of Stella's lemony tart personality.

Before Trix could answer, Pippa, Cara and Becka were beamed into the magic classroom and greeted with hoots, meows and a tiny squeak from Twitch.

"Oh, isn't it exiting!" Pippa exclaimed. Her high ponytail swished back and forth. She had a lavender ribbon in her hair that matched her familiar Twitch's fur and she wore a ruffled purple nightdress and fuzzy slippers.

"Isn't what exciting?" Cara asked as she scooped up Tabby. Cara's hair was twisted in a knot. She wore shorts and a T-shirt but her feet were bare.

"I don't know, but something's going on!" Pippa said, looking at each of her witchy friends. "Invitation and transportation and . . . I don't know, whatever other 'ations' we have yet to come."

"Maybe celebration," Becka said, as Sherlock landed on her shoulder. With his beak, he plaited her hair. Becka's baggy polka-dot pyjamas must have been hand-me-downs from one of her sisters. She looked very sleepy and a bit embarrassed when she noticed that both of her socks had holes in them.

"Maybe it's a magical sleepover," Trix said. Jinx liked the sound of that, but the truth was ten million times better. Oh, how he wished he could tell Trix, but it was Lulu's surprise and Trix would find out soon enough.

Suddenly the room grew dark. The girls squealed. Spots of light shimmered on the ceiling like a sky full of stars, and then they formed a message:

Fly to Witching Hill as fast as you can.
A surprise is waiting for you when you land.

The broomsticks the girls had created when they were learning to fly appeared, magically, in front of them. The familiars raced to their witches' besoms. Jinx kneaded his paws up and down on the bushy end of Trix's broom until his seat was just right, then he settled down and blinked up at Trix. He was ready to fly. He loved to fly. Next to birds, cats were the best co-pilots.

"Why would we go to Witching Hill?" Stella asked as the message faded away. A gleaming portal opened in the ceiling of the magic classroom so that they could see the real stars and the beautiful moon. "The only thing on Witching Hill is that terrible haunted house."

"Yuck!" Becka and Cara shrieked in unison.

"I don't want to get cobwebs in my hair," Cara said with a shiver.

The rosy pink left Becka's cheeks. "Y-y-you don't s-s-suppose there are g-g-ghosts up there, do you?" Becka stuttered. "I don't even like ghost stories."

Jinx and Trix shared a secret smile. They both knew that there was nothing spooky about the house on Witching Hill.

"I thought this was going to be fun," Stella complained. "Now I'm going to get my best pyjamas dirty." She began her favourite spell: "Sparkle, glitter, shimmer, shine." Jinx had heard Stella cast that spell lots of times. It was always about making her or her friends look pretty. Jinx liked to look nice, too. He gave his sparkling spots a lick. A kitten needs to look his best when he's going to a top-secret ball. He licked his front paw and smoothed it over his ears.

Oh, no! He'd missed the end of Stella's spell, and now a sparkly cloud was surrounding her. When the air cleared, Stella's pink pyjamas had transformed into a faded pair of pink jeans and a pink jacket with a hood. "I'm ready now."

The witches-in-training mounted their besoms. "Is everyone ready?" Trix asked. "Ready! Steady! Go!"

Each girl whispered her own special flying incantation and blasted off into the night sky. Jinx loved the rush of air through his fur. He hunched down and dug his claws into the broom. They flew higher and higher and faster and faster. Their magical adventure had begun!

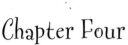

Chapter Four

Trix led the way to Magic Mansion. She looped through clouds and zigzagged around the treetops. The moon was casting a magical glow over Little Witching. All five girls, with their familiars perched proudly on the back of their brooms, formed a line and cut a path through a moonbeam. Trix thought they must look magically marvellous up here. She hoped that another young witch was looking out of her bedroom window somewhere and seeing them for the first time.

At last Trix spotted Magic Mansion high on Witching Hill. She squinted when she spotted a tall, thin chimney right in the centre of the roof. She had never noticed that before. As she flew closer, what she'd thought was a chimney changed shape. She would know those jingle-jangling bracelets and that silvery-white hair, black lace gown and witch's hat anywhere. It was Lulu!

Trix waved and her tummy went all butterflies and wiggly-worms. Lulu made *everything* more magical. And if they were going to Magic Mansion then it must be for something super-duper special!

"Magic up, my lovely witches and frightfully friendly familiars!" Lulu called as the witches landed on the roof around her. "Tonight is a very special night." Lulu clapped her hands and twirled, which set her bracelets jingle-jangling. "Tonight you will be tested by the Sisterhood of Magic. You will need to solve a series of puzzles and complete a series of magical tasks by midnight – the witching hour."

A test? Trix hated tests. She knew stuff. Of course she did, but the word *test* seemed to act like a rubber, randomly erasing information from her brain. She wasn't ready for a test. She hadn't studied for it. What if she didn't pass?

Lulu smiled at Trix as if she knew the bazillion worries that had invaded Trix's brain like aliens. "These puzzles and tasks will test what you've learned so far. For some tests, you will need to use magic, but for others all you will need is your brain. And if you are successful then you will receive an amazing surprise."

Trix generally liked surprises. She hoped Lulu meant the good kind of surprise because there were also bad surprises – like when her stinky little brother, Oscar, filled her water bottle with slimy pond water or when he *surprised* her with a nicely wrapped box of bugs. It had taken Trix and her best friend, Holly, two hours to free the bugs from her bedroom. And, even after three months, she still sometimes thought she saw creepy-crawlies in her room.

"We'd better get started," Lulu said, scanning the night sky. Dozens of witches on brooms were circling overhead and flying in from every direction. "New witches are travelling here from around the country for this enchanted exam."

Trix felt worried and happy at the same time. She knew there would be magic and, if Lulu was involved, fun, but she couldn't forget it was a test. She needed to make sure her brain was switched to maximum capacity. *Think! Think! Think!* she told herself.

"And, remember," Lulu said, with what Trix was sure was a cheeky grin, "you are in training to be fairy godmothers. And what do fairy godmothers do?"

"Grant wishes and help others!" the girls shouted together. They had each granted the wish of someone in Little Witching recently. Trix remembered how it felt to help someone else. It was like eating chocolate and laughing with her best friend rolled into one.

"OK, my future fairy godmothers," Lulu said and gathered them in a circle. "Here is your first riddle: *Sometimes bigger isn't better. Sometimes the way forwards is down, not up. And sometimes where there's smoke, there's flyer.*"

Lulu waved her arms above her head. The air was filled with the jingly sound of her bracelets and her laughter. "Good luck! Tootles!" she called as she disappeared in a puff of smoke. "See you at midnight!"

Trix wanted more than anything to be a fairy godmother one day. It was the highest honour the Sisterhood of Magic could bestow on a witch. She felt a tightness in her chest. That was the squeeze of hope and the fear of failure. Jinx brushed against her leg. Yes, she had to remember Jinx would be at her side to help her, but Trix's hope dimmed a smidge because she had absolutely no idea what Lulu's riddle meant.

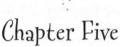

Chapter Five

"Oh, that riddle is easy-peasy!" Stella exclaimed and flicked her perfectly straightened hair over her shoulder.

"Is it?" Cara asked.

"Really?" Becka said. Both of their expressions showed that they were clueless.

"If you're so smart," Pippa said, putting her hands on her hips, "then why don't you tell us?"

Stella smiled, but it wasn't a friendly smile. Her smile stretched tight across her lips, and there was a mischievous twinkle in her eye. "I think it's every witch for herself," Stella said and whispered a spell. In a puff of pink smoke, Stella was gone.

All the remaining witches-in-training stared wide-eyed at each other.

Creeping cats! It was only the first riddle and Trix was stumped already.

"*I* don't think it's easy-peasy," Cara murmured and cuddled Tabby in her arms.

"I'm not very good at riddles," Becka confessed.

Pippa inched closer to Trix and whispered, "What do we do now?"

"Maybe if we work together we can solve Lulu's riddle," Trix suggested.

"Can we work with you?" Becka asked, hooking arms with Cara and coming closer to Trix and Pippa.

For a second, Trix wanted to say no. Cara and Becka hadn't always been nice to Trix and Pippa, and part of Trix wanted to be just a little mean back. Jinx crawled up the broom handle next to Trix and gave her a nudge with his nose. Jinx was right. If she didn't help Cara and Becka, then she was no better than Stella. Trix shuddered at the thought of being like Stella.

"Four heads are better than one," Trix said, climbing off her broom and waving the girls into a circle.

"I've got enough trouble with one head," Pippa giggled and knocked heads with Twitch, who was perched on her shoulder.

Trix's heart began to pound as if it were counting down the minutes to midnight. They were wasting time when they should be solving riddles. "OK, brains, start thinking!" she told her team.

"What did Lulu say again?" Becka asked.

Trix recalled Lulu's message word for word. She understood each word separately, but together they didn't make any sense. "I think we have to break it down sentence by sentence."

"Sometimes bigger isn't better," Pippa

repeated the first part of the riddle. "So that means smaller is better?"

"That's good, Pippa!" Trix exclaimed.

"And sometimes the way forwards is down, not up." Cara shook her head. "Oh, I don't know."

"This is hopeless," Becka said and curled the end of her plait around and around her finger.

"The last part is about smoke, isn't it?" Pippa asked.

Trix looked round for a clue. They were standing on a roof with nothing to see but the night sky and lots and lots of chimneys. Wait, that was it! "Chimneys!"

"Huh?" Becka and Cara said together.

"What comes out of chimneys?" Trix asked, but she already knew the answer.

"Smoke!" the girls replied.

"What was the last part of the riddle?" Trix asked the others. "Where there's smoke there's fire."

"No, she said *flyer*, not fire," Becka corrected.

Trix could feel the answer to the riddle bubbling up inside her. It was like watching a fuzzy picture coming into focus. "I think we need to shrink ourselves and fly down the chimneys!" Trix blurted. She smiled a big riddle-solving smile.

"Well done to all of us! We've solved it together." Pippa clapped as they all looked at the chimneys on the rooftop. There were big ones and small ones, skinny ones and fat ones. Some were square and some were strange shapes that Trix couldn't name.

"Good luck, everyone!" Trix said as the witches and their familiars climbed onto their besoms. But, just before she jetted off, she felt a pinch of doubt. She hoped their answer was right. She crossed her fingers and toes, which wasn't very witchy, but she needed all the luck she could get. "I'm going to need your help, Jinx."

Jinx sat up straight and wiggled his whiskers to give Trix's magic an extra boost. She recited a shrinking spell and watched the world grow bigger and bigger and bigger. The chimneys were now the size of trees.

"Creeping cats!" Trix squeaked as a firefly as big as a bird buzzed by. "This must be what it's like to be a bunny."

Jinx nodded.

A gust of wind tossed Trix's broom like a speck of dust in a super-suction vacuum cleaner. Trix spotted the source of the storm. Five young witches were zooming straight towards the roof.

"We'd better get going before we get squashed!" Trix told Jinx and her witchy friends. And, with that, Trix, Pippa, Cara and Becka each swooped into a different chimney.

"Hold on tight, Jinx!" Trix called as she

angled her broom down, down, down. She rubbed her eyes. It was getting darker and darker. Then, suddenly, the chimney began to glow.

Jinx's spots were sparkling and lighting the way. "Thanks, Jinx! You really are a star!"

And it was just in time . . . "Whoa!" Trix shouted as she steered her besom left and then sharply right. The chimney twisted and turned like a rollercoaster.

"Yippee!" Trix shouted as her stomach flipped with each loopity-loop. She and Jinx stayed glued to the broom like expert pilots. Maybe this was part of the test too. If so, she was passing with flying colours.

She squinted to get a better look at what was coming

up fast in front of her. "I need maximum sparkle, Jinx!" Trix shouted.

Her furry little kitten was now glowing as bright as a spotlight, and that's when Trix realised that something was blocking the chimney.

"Creeping ca-ca-ca-cats!" Trix screamed as she skidded to a stop.

But she didn't react fast enough. She swept Jinx into her arms, squeezed her eyes shut and braced herself for impact.

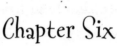

Chapter Six

Jinx huddled up close to Trix and waited for the OUCH that was bound to come. But, instead of being slammed into something hard, Jinx and Trix were squished into something pillowy and soft. They bounced back with a BOING.

Trix eased her broom closer to the pudgy pink mass. Jinx extended his paw and poked, softly at first but then a bit harder. He dug his tiny claws in to see if he could dig a way through.

"Ouch!"

Jinx looked at Trix, but she hadn't uttered a word.

Trix prodded the pinkness with her broom.

"Cut it out! That hurts!"

Jinx would recognise that whine anywhere.

"Stella?" Trix called, and stifled a giggle. Normal-sized Stella was stuck in the chimney.

Stella let out an exasperated sigh. "Why did it have to be Trix who found me?"

"I can hear you, you know." Trix put her broom in reverse. "And I could leave you here if I wanted."

Jinx rolled with laughter. It would serve Stella right.

"Shhhh…" Trix told Jinx.

Yes, she was right. It wasn't nice to laugh when someone got themselves into a super-silly situation. Jinx clamped his front paws over his mouth, but his whiskers twitched with stifled laughter.

"Well, are you going to help me or not?" Stella demanded. The pink mass in front of them wiggled and grey ash rained down on Trix and Jinx.

"Keep still, Stella!" Trix called. "How did you get stuck anyway?"

"I knew the riddle meant that we needed to go down the chimney," Stella explained. "I knew that straight away, faster than the rest of you. So I cast a spell to quickly send me down the chimney, which it did. It's just that this is as far as I got."

"The riddle meant for us to SHRINK and fly down the chimney," Trix said.

"I know that now, silly," Stella spat out the words as if they tasted sour in her mouth.

Jinx was very proud of Trix. She had worked out the right answer to the first riddle. Stella was fast, but not accurate, and you needed to be both – obviously.

Rascal barked.

"Is Rascal OK?" Trix asked.

"Yeah, we're both fine. Just stuck. Get us out of here." Even when Stella was asking for help, she still sounded mean.

Trix smiled mischievously. "What's the magic word?"

"Don't you think I've tried magic?" Stella snorted. "But I couldn't think of a single word to rhyme with shrink, except stink, and that spell didn't turn out so well either. I was just about to—"

"No, Stella," Trix interrupted. "I mean the magic WORD."

Jinx sniggered again. He'd heard Trix's mum say it a million times to Oscar. The magic word was . . .

"Please!" Stella sort of barked.

"I guess that's the best we're going to get from her," Trix muttered to Jinx.

Jinx nodded and pointed to Trix's big green watch. He needed to remind Trix of Lulu's midnight deadline. Jinx didn't know how to tell the time, but he knew they were spending too long with Stella.

"Oh, right, we do need to get going." Trix crinkled up her nose as if something smelled bad. Jinx was sure that part of Trix didn't really want to help Stella, but that was one of the many lovely things about Trix. It was in her nature to help others. She was going to make a wonderful fairy godmother one day.

Trix pointed to Stella and repeated her shrinking spell. Jinx wiggled his whiskers to give Trix's rhyme a magical boost.

Down, down, down shrank Stella and Rascal. Jinx wiggled his whiskers again. The smaller Stella was, the better. Stella and Rascal shrank to the same size as Trix and Jinx and then they kept on shrinking. Trix held out her hand to catch the teeny, tiny pair. They landed with a plop in the palm of her hand.

"Hey, what's going on?" tiny Stella squeaked. Rascal barked, but it sounded more like the EEK EEK of a little mouse.

Jinx could see in Trix's eyes that she knew what he had done, but she didn't scold. "I guess my magic is more powerful than I realised," Trix said. "What happened to your broom?"

"It got smashed when Rascal and I got crunched in the chimney," Stella replied.

"I'll take us the rest of the way." Trix carefully placed the pair on Jinx's back. Jinx could feel little tugs on his fur as tiny Stella and little Rascal held on.

Stella muttered something into Jinx's fur.

"What did you say?" Trix asked.

"I said," Stella paused and gulped as if the words were stuck in her throat. "I said thank you."

That was its own kind of magic, Jinx thought. He couldn't remember the last time Stella had said thank you to anyone. Trix should get extra credit for that amazing trick!

And off they went. They zoomed through the chimney. Jinx turned his spots to maximum sparkle again to guide the way. Stella screamed and pulled at Jinx's fur with every twist and turn.

Suddenly a dark cloud enveloped them.

"What's going on?" Stella shouted.

Trix kept her cool. She slowed down and steered her broom very carefully. Then they burst forwards, riding a powerful gust of wind as they were spat out of the chimney and tumbled onto the floor.

"What have you done?" Stella moaned. "Look at

me. My outfit is ruined. Where are we? Did you even go the right way?" On and on she complained. Jinx tuned out her voice. He looked around. There were no doors or windows, just an old stone fireplace and a smoky room.

"Do I have to do everything?" Stella asked and recited a spell that made the witches and familiars pop back to their normal sizes. "We need to hurry. I mean, how are we ever going to finish this ridiculous test by midnight? Did you have to be so slow?" Stella dusted herself off.

Jinx and Rascal raced around the room, inspecting every nook and cranny. Stella may be irritating, but she was right about one thing. They were trapped in a room with no means of escape and the clock was counting down.

Chapter Seven

"Congratulations, my lovely witches!" It was Lulu's voice, but Lulu was nowhere to be seen. "All my witches have passed their first test with flying besoms! Prepare for the next riddle. It's a bit befuddling so be sure to use your feet." Lulu laughed. "I mean, your heads, of course."

"Look!" Trix pointed at the floor near the chimney. Words were appearing in the

ash. Trix spotted the words *Cinderella* and *dancing*. Next came a few numbers, first *two* and then *one*.

"What does it mean?" Trix asked, stepping closer as the words formed sentences. Jinx and Rascal sniffed at the words as if they were trying to read them too.

"That's for me to know and you to find out," Stella said. "*Left, right, up and down,*" she pointed to the message and chanted, "*Mix the words all around.*"

The words shifted so that the sentences no longer made sense. Stella scooped up Rascal and muttered something in his ear. Then she did a little happy dance and disappeared.

"Seriously?" Trix shouted to the four walls

and the ceiling and floor too. She couldn't believe that Stella had tricked her again. The girl would never be a fairy godmother – unless she changed her entire personality. Trix stomped around the room. She was angry with herself for having trusted Stella.

Then she took a deep breath and tried to calm down. She could spend her time being frustrated with Stella or she could try to somehow solve the riddle. She closed her eyes and tried to visualise the magical message in the ash. It had had something to do with Cinderella. If she concentrated, she could kind of – sort of – see the words in her mind.

Clank! Rattle! Bang!

Trix's eyelids sprang open. Something was in the chimney. Jinx jumped into Trix's arms as whatever it was began to scream.

Trix imagined what might live in a dark old chimney. Maybe they'd disturbed a sleeping soot monster!

Bang! Bump! Yeow!

Trix hugged Jinx closer, and he cuddled her right back.

Quack! Quack!

Quack? Trix and Jinx stared at each other in confusion. Plumes of smoke billowed from the fireplace. Whatever was in the chimney was coming out.

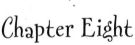

Chapter Eight

The smoke cleared and an ash-covered image began to take shape. It wasn't a witch-eating were-beast or a snaggle-toothed tiger. It shook from the top of its two bushy bunches to the toes of its curly-tipped slippers. It wasn't an *it* at all. It was a girl about the same age as Trix.

"Dirty and dusty will never do," the girl said.

The girl was a witch, and she was casting a spell.

"I need to be tidy to get the next blue."

Blue? The ash in the room changed from a smoky grey to the colour of juicy blueberries.

The girl giggled. "Oh, I'm always doing splat, hat, THAT!" She repeated her spell again and this time filled in the right word – *clue*. A gentle breeze blew through the room, whisking away the dirt. Trix could now see that the girl had blonde, almost white, hair tied in two lopsided bunches. Her nightdress was sky-blue and covered with moons and stars.

"Have you seen a duck anywhere around here?" she asked as she searched the room. "That duck would get lost in a fish tank." She froze. "Did you hear that?"

Trix shook her head. She hadn't heard anything. "I'm Trix and this is Jinx," she began. "Maybe we can—"

The girl held up her hands as if projecting a forcefield. "One sec-o-rama." She tilted her head and squinted. "Listen."

Trix heard it that time –
rustling and quacking. A
duck flew from the
chimney in a flutter of
feathers and quacks.

"Oh, there you are!"
the girl said as the duck
waddled over to her.
"This is Quackers and
I'm Louise, or Lou for
short."

"Nice to meet you," Trix
said. She couldn't help but smile.
There was something about Lou that was
super-duper likeable.

Jinx jumped to the
floor and raced over
to greet Quackers,
touching his nose to
Quackers' bill. They
seemed to be instant
friends.

"We'd better get quacking," Lou said.
"Never waste time unless you can make it!"

That sounded so familiar. Where had Trix heard that phrase before?

"That's what my great, great, groovy Aunt Pearl always used to say," Lou said with a nervous laugh. "What's the next piddle, diddle, RIDDLE?"

"Well, the words are here, but the riddle's a bit mixed up." Trix pointed to the message Stella had scrambled.

Lou squinted at the words in the ash. "Why are the words muddled up?"

"It's a long story that ends with a punch line of *Stella*," Trix said. Lou was lucky and didn't know Stella. Trix didn't want to waste her breath explaining Stella's dirty tricks. "But never mind that. It's something to do with Cinderella."

"I'm pretty good at unscrambling things," Lou said. "Aren't I, Quackers?" Quackers quacked and nodded. "Maybe we can sort this out together. Two heads are better than ton, fun, ONE!" Lou giggled. "You know what I mean."

"One! That's it!" Trix exclaimed. She

pointed to each word as she put the riddle back together again. "*Cinderella had one. But it's better with two*." The words re-ordered themselves as Trix spoke. "*For dancing and running, the pair must suit you*."

Trix guessed the answer just as Lou said, "It must be shoes."

Lou hooked her arm in Trix's and began to spin them around and around. "Aren't you a clever log!" Lou said.

"I think you mean clever *clogs*," Trix laughed.

They must have solved the riddle correctly because the room crackled with magic and the girls and their familiars vanished into thin air.

Chapter Nine

Ker-splat!

Trix, Jinx, Lou and Quackers were dumped into a lumpy pile of . . .

Trix couldn't believe her eyes. They had landed on hundreds – no, millions – no, squillions – of *shoes*. Maybe this was the shoe cupboard belonging to a human-sized centipede with hundreds of legs. That thought made Trix shiver.

"I've never seen so many shoes," Lou said.

Trix picked up a neon-blue sandal and then a black boot with a pink stripe. That's when she realised her slippers were missing. Magic Mansion really was magical. If it had an entire room for shoes, Trix's brain marvelled at what else she might find here.

Lou picked up a green plimsoll and a purple polka-dot pump and slipped them on. "I love these!" she said, kicking her feet in the air.

"Those are gorgeous," Trix said and snatched a flowered wellie and a red shoe with a jewelled heel. She limped around in her mismatched shoes. "Look at me!"

The girls tried on shoe after shoe – fancy ones and plain ones, dainty ones and clunky ones. Trix often wore one black and one white trainer. She liked to mix things that most people didn't think belonged together. "Try these!" Trix handed Lou one silver and one gold shoe, both with high heels.

Lou tried them on and toppled over with a giggle. "Do you think we'll ever be able to walk in high heels?"

Trix shrugged. She preferred trainers to heels – one fire-engine red and one candyfloss pink to be exact. She pulled on the shoes and danced around.

"Trix," Lou said as she laced up a boot. "What are we doing here?"

Trix was having so much fun trying on shoes that she had forgotten about her witchy test and the midnight deadline. She checked her watch. It was nearly eleven o'clock. She climbed up the nearest shoe hill to get a better look around. "What did the riddle say?"

"Something about two shoes being better than one," Lou replied.

Trix studied the piles and piles of shoes. "Do you notice something strange about these shoes?" Trix held up one shoe and then another.

Lou stopped pulling on a yellow flipper. "Come to think of it, I don't see a *pair* of shoes anywhere."

"I think we are supposed to find a matching pair of shoes," Trix said. "The right ones for us."

"Oh, good, I love shoe shopping!" Lou hopped and Quackers flew around the pile of shoes, searching for a matching pair.

"Jinx, where are you?" Trix's familiar was missing again.

A green and white trainer began to quiver and quake. Maybe that was the shoe for her. The trainer hopped out of the pile.

Meow! It was Jinx, wearing the trainer like a hat.

"You silly kitten," Trix said and gave Jinx a friendly stroke. "You've got to help me find the right pair of shoes."

Jinx scampered down the mountain of shoes and raced from pile to pile. Trix sort of surfed down the shoes, causing an avalanche of footwear. She landed on the floor with a bump.

Meow! Meow! Jinx called.

Trix raced over to Jinx. He'd found the perfect shoe for her. It was silvery-pink with a bow on the toe. She'd always wanted a pretty pair of shoes just like that.

The air around them began to spark and then Becka, Pippa and Cara, followed swiftly by Twitch, Tabby and Sherlock, magically materialised in the room.

Trix slipped on her shoe and hobbled over to greet her now shoeless friends. "All you need to do is find a matching pair of shoes!" Trix said. "At least, I think that's what we're supposed to do."

The girls didn't waste a minute. They tunnelled though the stacks of shoes.

"Got mine!" Becka called as her owl, Sherlock, brought her the twin of the shiny black shoe Becka was wearing. Once she had both shoes on, her toes started tapping. "These shoes are magical! They're taking me somew-w-where!" Becka squealed as she started to walk and then run. "The shoes are carrying me away." She raced off in a fit of giggles.

Quack! Quack! Quackers was leading Lou through the shoes back to Trix.

"Pippa and Cara, this is my new friend, Lou!" Trix introduced the familiars too.

"I need a black hoot, loot, BOOT," Lou said and held up one sequined lace-up boot.

Pippa chose a pink ballerina slipper with long silk ribbons. "I've always wanted a pair like this."

Cara liked a green-and-yellow striped pair of pumps. Trix pointed her toe to display her pink shoe. "Let's spread out and look for each other's shoes," she suggested.

"Our familiars can help," Pippa added. Jinx dashed over to Trix and wiggled his whiskers.

"Great idea," Lou said. "Ready! Steady! Go!"

The girls set out in different directions. In no time the witches and familiars had spotted the missing shoes – except the one to match Trix's.

Cara twirled in her stripy shoes and raced away.

Pippa and Lou wore one shoe and carried the other.

"You should put your shoes on," Trix told her friends.

"No!" Pippa and Lou said in unison.

"We'll wait for you to find your perfect pair," Pippa said.

"Don't be silly! I don't want you to be late. I know my shoe is around here somewhere. Me and Super Jinx will sniff it out, won't we, Jinx?"

Jinx nodded and darted away to inspect another pile.

"Go on!" Trix urged the girls.

Lou and Pippa slipped on their shoes. "Trix, you are duper-super dice, twice, NICE!" Lou said as the girls' legs began to run.

"Good luck!" Trix shouted, but suddenly she felt a bit nervous about being left behind.

"See you soooooooon!" Pippa called as she lunged ahead and then her voice faded away.

Trix hobbled from pile to pile. Now she knew what Cinderella must have felt like, running from the ball with only one glass slipper.

"Aaaaaaghhhh!"

Trix looked up just as a flash of pink tumbled down the nearest pile of shoes.

"Don't just stand there," Stella called, "help me up."

Trix hesitated for a moment. She couldn't believe she was helping Stella again, but then she shoved shoes and boots and sandals aside.

As Trix helped Stella to her feet, both the girls exclaimed, "My shoe!" and pointed to each other's feet. Stella was wearing the partner to Trix's pink shoe.

"This shoe?" Stella kicked her foot high in the air. "This shoe found *my* foot, so we are clearly meant to be together. Anyway, I don't have time to find another pair," Stella whined.

Stella was right. Time was running out. "Please, Stella," Trix begged. "For once in your life, be nice."

"*Sparkle, glitter, shimmer, shine,*" Stella started.

Oh, no! Trix dropped to the floor and hugged the shoe to her chest, hoping to shield it from Stella's magic. "You are not getting my shoe!" she cried, begging her brain to think of a spell. Shoe. True. Blue. New. Rhyming words flew through her head. She sounded like Lou. But it was too late.

"*Give me the shoe because it's mine!*" Stella finished her spell. The shoe wriggled from Trix's grasp and danced over to Stella.

Chapter Ten

Stella slowly slipped on the shoe. "See you later, Trixie." Then she added, "Maybe."

Jinx crouched down, a low growl humming in his throat. He would snatch Trix's shoes back. He pounced at Stella's feet, but he landed on the floor with a SPLAT as the shoes raced away with her.

Anger flashed through Jinx like a thunderbolt. Every hair on his cat body rose, so that he appeared nearly twice his normal size. His tail flicked in the air and twitched with anger. He would not let Stella win. He raced around the room inspecting every shoe, but he couldn't find two shoes that matched each other and Trix's bubbly personality. He skidded to a stop at Trix's wiggling toes.

"It's OK, Jinx," Trix said, smoothing his fur and his temper with a long stroke from the tip of his pink nose to the top of his black tail. Jinx leaned into her touch and completely forgot about nasty Stella.

"I have an idea, but I may need some magical help," Trix said. "Whiskers at the ready, Jinx."

Jinx perked up. He wiggled his whiskers on one side, and waggled his whiskers on the other. He was ready for whatever magic Trix wanted to weave.

Trix cleared her throat. "High heels or trainers, I really don't care," Trix sing-songed. "I need two matching shoes to wear." Jinx double- and triple-wiggled his whiskers, magically boosting Trix's spell.

A low rumble hummed in the distance. Jinx pricked his ears and tuned in to the sound. What was it? It sounded like scattered raindrops on the roof. The drumming grew louder, as if the spring sprinkle had turned into a downpour.

Shoes were leaping out of the piles and meeting their matches in mid-air. The pairs of shoes formed a line that marched two-by-two straight towards Jinx. He dodged out of the way. The shoes stopped with a final clip-clop in front of Trix.

"Creeping cats!" Trix exclaimed. "So many shoes to choose from." Trix knew immediately which shoes were meant to be hers. She pointed to a pair of rainbow ballet flats, and they instantly materialised on her feet. Jinx scampered over to inspect the shoes. They twinkled with a thousand dazzling jewels. Jinx sniffed and sneezed. The magical shoes tickled his nose.

Trix's toes began to tap. With each tippity-tap the shoes changed colour. First one shoe was purple and the other pink. Then they turned two different shades of blue. On and on they cycled through every colour Trix had ever seen or imagined. They were the perfect shoes for Trix.

"Hey, wait!" Trix yelled at the shoes as they carried her off, feet first.

Jinx raced along beside her. He pounced on one shoe, but it flicked him off. He jumped on the other and wrapped his paws around Trix's ankle. The shoes whirled right out of the shoe room and into a long corridor that stretched as far as his yellow eyes could see. Doors of every shape, colour and size lined the corridor.

Meow! This was fun.

"You're right, Jinx!" Trix said, catching him when the shoes did a few high kicks. "This IS fun!"

As they danced down the corridor, doors opened to reveal many strange and wonderful sights. There was a door that opened onto a jungle. The next room was full of bouncing balls. Another door swung open to reveal a room made entirely of sweets; the sticky smell of toasted marshmallows filled the air. Jinx squirmed in Trix's arms when they passed a room full of monkeys playing table tennis. Oh, how he wanted to play too! But the Sisterhood of Magic Ball would be even more fun than a room full of monkeys. He couldn't wait until Trix learned Lulu's secret surprise.

Magic Mansion was a maze of corridors. Jinx was glad the shoes were leading the way.

"What's happening?" Trix said as her shoes sprouted wings. She flew up a flight of stairs and then skated down another. "This place is too big inside for its outside."

Jinx understood what his witch meant. So many rooms couldn't possibly fit into the house on top of Witching Hill.

"I suppose they don't call it Magic Mansion for nothing!" Trix giggled.

And then Trix and Jinx saw them at the same time – up ahead were two massive metal doors. Jinx thought they looked like something from a haunted house or a dungeon. They were heading straight for the doors, and Trix's shoes showed no signs of stopping.

At the very last minute, the doors creaked open and Trix's pace slowed to a walk. Inside were rows and rows of bookcases, similar to the ones in the magic classroom, and in the middle of the room were several tables. Around each table sat more witches-in-training.

"This looks like a science lab," Trix whispered to Jinx, and she was right. There were vials and test tubes and gadgets everywhere.

"Hey, Trix!" It was Lou and Pippa. "Over here!" they called, and waved.

Trix's shoes stopped, but Trix's body didn't. She and Jinx tumbled to the floor.

Pippa and Lou rushed to Trix's side and helped her up.

"It's about time you joined us!" snapped Stella. She kicked up her shoes, which used to be Trix's.

Trix didn't say a word. She tiptoed next to Lou and Pippa, making sure that Stella got a good long look at her beautiful rainbow shoes.

"Welcome, Trixibelle Morgan!"

Jinx looked up to see the most sparkly and twinkly witch of them all. Magic created a buzzy glow all around her.

"I'm the Headmistress of the Sisterhood of Magic," the sparkly witch said. "In here we are carrying out a test of creativity, kindness and magic. The other girls have already started. Now, you must whip up your very own Party Pretty Potion."

That would be easy-peasy for Jinx's oh-so-talented witch. Potions were basic magic. Then Jinx remembered that Trix's first potion had gone haywire. Her Happiness Potion had made Holly disappear!

Jinx leaped down and began to inspect the ingredients on a nearby shelf. There was a glowing jar, which Jinx thought might be the shimmer of the moon, and another that could be the ripple of the sea.

"Party Pretty Potions are generally used to help one look particularly pretty for a special occasion. You must complete your potion," the Headmistress extended her hand in front of her to reveal an old-fashioned hourglass, "before the last grain of sand passes through this hourglass." The sand was already falling. Jinx watched a golden grain squeeze through with a POP, followed by another, and then another. Jinx thought they sounded like bubbles popping. Time was elapsing at an alarming rate.

"Good luck!" the Headmistress said.

Trix looked around at all the witches already pouring and stirring their potions. She was going to need lots of luck because she was already way behind everyone else.

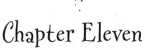

Chapter Eleven

Bookcases stretched from floor to ceiling, filled with jars that glowed and swirled and shivered and oozed and shook. Trix's brain was suddenly buzzing too. There were so many possibilities.

"A Party Pretty Potion! Do you think that means we are going to a party?" Pippa whispered to Trix.

Trix felt giddy with excitement at the

thought of a party at Magic Mansion. "I hope so!"

Pippa's face scrunched into a frown. "I can't think of anything pretty." Pippa hadn't even started her potion.

"You're great at potions," Trix said, and Pippa was. She had easily memorised the ingredients on Lulu's bookcase. Oh, how Trix wished Lulu was here to help.

"Yes, but I'm not very good with timers," Pippa said. "I get nervous."

"Don't think about the hourglass," Trix said and turned Pippa so she couldn't see the sand draining away. Trix had to agree, though. The *pop, pop, popping* was distracting. "You know pretty and you know potions!"

"You're right, Trix," Pippa said and gave her a hug. "Where do you think they keep their midnight glow and stardust?"

As if Pippa's lavender familiar Twitch understood, he pointed his wiry tail and raced off. "Follow that rat!" Trix laughed.

Midnight glow and stardust certainly sounded pretty. Trix wished she could think what to put in her potion.

"My potion is bound to be the best!" Stella exclaimed from her place a few tables away. "I am the prettiest witch, after all." She magicked up a mirror and admired herself. "Pretty is my speciality," she said to everyone around her. Stella was always casting pretty spells. Trix knew she would ace this portion of the test.

Crash!

Trix and the other witches turned towards the source of the sound. Lou stood red-faced surrounded by broken jars. A thick goo bubbled at her feet. "Oops!" Lou said nervously.

"Ew, gross," Stella moaned and pinched her nose. "That stinks! How are those ingredients ever going to be pretty?"

"Don't listen to her," Trix told Lou. "She's mean to everyone."

"I can fix this," Lou said. "I know a super fix-it spell."

"*Gross and disgusting do not mix.*" Lou smiled at Trix. "*Messes are messy so I need a trix, nix, FIX.*"

Trix smiled back, although she was thinking that Lou was even worse than she was at casting spells. But Lou's spell worked! The goo separated into four piles, the shards of glass re-formed, and the ingredients snaked back into their appropriate jars.

"What are you going to put in your potion?" Trix asked as she helped Lou place her jars on the table. She sneaked a peek at one of the labels – *Dandelion Petals*. Dandelions weren't the prettiest flowers, but they were beautiful in their own special way.

"I'm putting the things I like best into my potion." Lou shook a jar that clanked with copper coins. "I love shiny pennies." She held up two eggs. "And scrambled eggs are my favourite breakfast." She cracked the eggs and swished them around in her bowl.

"*Eggs*, really?" Stella said as she brushed by their table, carrying a bouquet of roses and a glowing jar marked *Sunset*.

Lou's shoulders sagged. "What do I know about pretty?"

"Don't listen to Stella," Trix told Lou. "Your idea is a good one. If we all agreed on what was pretty – well, we'd all look and dress the same, and what fun would that be?"

"You're right," Lou said, brightening, and she got back to work. The other witches were also busy collecting ingredients and mixing potions. Pippa was helping another witch mix her potion. Trix thought Pippa would make a wonderful fairy godmother one day.

But, right now, Trix needed to focus. "Jinx, what's the prettiest thing you can think of?" she asked.

Jinx's tail flicked left and then right as if he were thinking, and then he sprang to his back legs and held his front paws out wide. He wibbled and wobbled on his back legs as he flapped his front paws.

"Oh, you are a clever cat!" Trix exclaimed. Somehow she knew exactly what Jinx meant. "Butterflies are the prettiest creatures in the world!"

Trix found a jar of butterfly scales straight away and poured them into a bowl.

Lou opened a jar and the air was tainted with the most terrible smell. Trix had to pinch her nose. Whatever was in there smelled worse than Oscar's socks. Lou laughed. "I like stinky cheese."

"I think that's a really . . ." Trix paused and crossed her fingers behind her back. A little white lie wasn't bad if it saved someone's feelings. "A really interesting choice," Trix finished.

At least Lou had nearly finished her potion, even if it was a bit strange. Trix was only just beginning hers.

"Oh, I forgot my favourite thing," Lou said.

Trix wasn't sure if she wanted to know what that was.

"Sherbet lemons!" Lou called as she raced away. Trix's cheeks puckered at the thought.

Trix tapped her foot as she tried to think of more pretty things to put in her potion. Her shoes changed from red to orange to yellow to green to blue to indigo and violet – all the colours of the rainbow. That was it! Rainbows were definitely pretty. That could be another ingredient in her potion.

She glanced at the hourglass. It was almost empty. She didn't have time to run around searching each shelf for ingredients. She'd have to try another spell. She winked at Jinx and he wiggled his whiskers as she said, *"Butterflies flutter. Rainbows glow. I need more colour. One, two, three, GO!"*

Two jars came zooming off the shelves and landed on the table right in front of Trix. She read the labels – *Rainbow Dew* and *Chameleon Pigment.* Would three ingredients be enough for a powerful potion?

Pop! Pop! Pop! Time was running out.

Trix tipped a few drops of chameleon pigment onto the butterfly scales and topped it off with rainbow dew. Jinx dipped his paw in the bowl and swished it around. Trix crossed her fingers and toes for extra luck.

"Three . . . two . . . one!" the other witches called as the final grains of sand drained away.

Trix had finished in the nick of time! "Thanks, Jinx!" Trix raised her hand, and Jinx gave her a high five with his paw.

The Headmistress floated overhead. "Well done, my lovely little witches." She had the most beautiful voice. When she spoke it was as if she were singing a song. "Now,

I have a little surprise. If you become fairy godmothers one day, you will be givers of smiles and granters of wishes." She waved her arms as if she were a hummingbird, hovering over a bloom. *"This and that. Here and there. Switch your potions. It's nice to share!"*

All the witches' potions floated in the air and then zoomed around the room.

"No!" Stella shouted as she tried to chase her potion. "I want *my* potion . . ." Her whine faded when she saw the Headmistress glaring at her. "I mean . . ." Stella's face flushed, "I am happy for another witch to have the best Party Pretty Potion ever."

Stella's potion was sprinkled over Lou. In a flash, Lou's nightdress transformed into the most glorious gown Trix had ever seen. As much as she hated to admit it, Stella's potion was amazing. The dress was a fiery red and it fitted Lou perfectly.

"No!" Stella grumbled as Trix's potion was sprinkled over her. "I can't look." Stella shut her eyes, but her jeans and jacket changed into a sophisticated gown that shimmered with every colour of the rainbow.

"You look beautiful," Lou told Stella.

And she did. Trix's potion had created a dress that swirled even when Stella was standing still. Trix beamed with pride.

Stella opened one eye and then the other. Her eyes widened in surprise. "It's . . . it's . . ." Stella stammered.

"Amazing," Lou finished the thought for Stella.

Stella nodded. "Thanks, Trix."

Trix felt the zing she always felt when she helped others – even Stella.

All around her, fellow witches were having magical makeovers. Not only were they wearing gowns fit for Cinderella's ball, but their hair was being styled as if they were getting ready for a fashion photo shoot.

Then Lou's stinky potion tipped out over Trix's head. Trix was prepared to be plonked by pennies and covered in cheese. But instead she found herself wearing a dress that was the colour of sunshine and glowed with its own light.

"I love it!" Trix said and hugged Lou.

Trix twirled in her new dress. Then she picked up Jinx and danced around the room. But her feet got tangled up and she tripped, losing one of her shoes, just as the Headmistress called, "It's time for your final test!" All the witches and their familiars disappeared, leaving one of Trix's beautiful rainbow shoes behind.

Chapter Twelve

In the blink of an eye, Trix found herself standing in a massive cellar with all the other witches and their familiars. It was cold and damp and smelled like earth, but that wasn't the strangest thing. The room looked like a mix between an antique shop and a junk yard. Trix and Jinx dodged out of the way as an old-fashioned box kite came floating down.

Jinx hopped
around, inspecting
everything. *Meow!* he
called when he came nose to beak with a
stuffed pterodactyl.

Everywhere Trix looked, she spotted
something she'd never seen before. There was
a lamp that looked like ladybirds whizzing
around a tree. A big wooden elephant had
golden Easter baskets hanging off each tusk.
There were buckets of tangled necklaces and
tubs of bracelets. Trix spotted a tarnished silver
tea set, the pot and cups filled with buttons.

"Surprise!"

"Aaaaaghhhhh!" Trix shrieked as someone
jumped out from behind an antique wardrobe.

Trix shook her head and stared. She
couldn't believe her eyes. "Aunt Belle?"

"Are you surprised?" Aunt Belle hugged

her favourite niece. Trix loved that her aunt looked part rock star and part fashion model. She had short spiky hair with electric-blue streaks that matched her stunning sequined gown. Trix was named after her Aunt Trixibelle, but Trix used the beginning of their name and Belle used the end. Not only did Aunt Belle share Trix's name, but she was also Trix's magical mentor. Until recently, Trix had had no idea that her aunt was really a witch.

"What are you doing here?" Trix asked.

"Your mentor gets to give you your last challenge," Aunt Belle explained. "You are doing very well so far, Trix."

Trix tucked her bare foot under her gown. She didn't want her aunt to see that she was missing a shoe. Someone bumped into her from behind. She turned to find Lou looking a bit sad.

"What's the matter?" Trix asked.

"I'm not sure what I'm supposed to do," Lou said. "Everyone else has a mentor, but I can't find my mentor anywhere." Lou's eyes brimmed with tears.

"You can share my mentor," Trix said and put an arm around Lou's shoulders. "Is that OK, Aunt Belle?"

"The more the merrier," Aunt Belle said. She pulled the girls in close. "You have shoes and gowns but you need something to top it all off. You must now use your magical powers to transform this junk into gems, and then magic the gems into a tiara."

"Why?" Trix asked, looking around at all the crazy stuff.

"It's what fairy godmothers do," Aunt Belle said. "We see something beautiful in everyone we meet, so this will be your *crowning* achievement." She winked. "Good luck and see you at midnight!" And with that, Aunt Belle was gone.

"We should probably get started," Lou said, grabbing an ornament from a nearby shelf. "Turning this into something pretty will be a chalice."

Trix guessed that Lou meant *challenge*. She was getting used to unscrambling riddles.

Lou held up a stone gargoyle. Jinx hissed

and Quackers quacked at it. Its smushed face was missing an eye and one of its ears had broken off. It looked like a cross between a dinosaur and a clown.

"It's sort of funny *and* scary." Trix squinted at the ugly thing. She couldn't imagine who would want such a weird statue in their house.

Lou tiled her head this way and that, admiring the gargoyle. "I can't remember how to transform things," she admitted.

"My tutor, Lulu, says that the key to transformations is to imagine the outcome you want," Trix explained as she tried to remember the rest of that particular magical lesson. "Lulu gave us an all-purpose transformation spell."

"What was it?" Lou asked.

Trix tried to remember. Her brain was crammed with thoughts and memories and ideas. Maybe it was the pressure of time or of the test, but Lulu's all-purpose transformation spell was buried too deep in her messy mind, and she couldn't remember it!

"Maybe we should come up with a rhyme of

our own," Trix said. Lou's face was wrinkled in confusion. "I'm pretty good at rhyming. Let's think of sparkly words that rhyme."

Lou bounced on her toes. "Magically marvellous!"

Trix cocked her head and studied Lou. That's what Lulu always said.

"I'll go first," Lou volunteered. "Sparkle. Quarkle. Narkle. Warkle. Zarkle. Farkle."

"Those are fun words," Trix said encouragingly. They rhymed, of course, but they were mostly nonsense words. How could she get Lou to understand that they needed *real* words for their spell? "Why don't I have a go?" Trix said. "Jewel, cruel, tool, rule, fool."

"Those are great rhymes. Let's use one on this!" Lou held up a rusty wrench. "*You rusty old tool, don't be cruel. I need to rule, so become a cruel, rule, JEWEL*." Lou glared at the wrench. Nothing happened.

"Let me try," Trix said. She thought for a moment about what she wanted to do and what words might be right. "*You must have been a useful tool, but now become a sparkling jewel,"* she chanted.

In a shimmer of glitter, the rusty wrench transformed. Lou was now holding the biggest diamond Trix had ever seen.

"Wow! You're plate, late, GREAT," Lou said and handed the stone to Trix.

"No, you keep it. You found the wrench," Trix told her. She checked the time on her big green watch. It was almost midnight! She wanted to help Lou but, at this rate, neither of them would finish in time. "Maybe we can come up with one rhyme that will work on everything we find."

"Oh, that sounds really clever," Lou said. Quackers flapped. There was something in his beak. Lou took it from him. "Quackers has found the top of a ketchup bottle. Thanks, Quack!"

"Beauty is everywhere," Trix started and nodded to Lou.

"Don't be a fool," Lou continued.

That was a good start, Trix thought. Maybe this spell would work. *"Find the beauty in junk and turn it into a jewel.*"

The girls, Jinx and Quackers stared at the ketchup top. It sputtered and sparked and . . .

"Wow!" Lou sighed. "That's a truly beautiful gem." She held it out to Trix. "You take it."

Trix brushed it away. "It's yours."

"But time is running out," Lou said.

"Maybe we can both make it if we hurry," Trix replied, searching for the next item.

"How about this?" Lou reached for an old fizzy-drink can but, as she thrust it at Trix, its rusty contents sloshed onto Trix's dress.

"Oh, no! I'll just . . ." Lou wiped at the dress, but that only made the stain bigger.

Trix's beautiful dress was ruined. "It's OK," Trix said, even though it wasn't. Her sunny yellow dress had a big brown blob right down the front. Trix stepped back from Lou.

RIIIIIIIIIIIIIIP!

Trix hadn't realised that Lou was standing on her dress. As she'd moved away, her lovely new gown had ripped right up the front, leaving a huge tear that showed Trix's knobbly knees.

"I am so sorry," Lou said. "Maybe I can use a spell to fix it."

Somewhere in Magic Mansion a clock began to strike.

Bong!

"It's midnight!" Trix gasped. There wasn't enough time to repair her dress and pass the test. She whispered their spell at the can. It transformed into a fiery red ruby. "At least one of us can finish in time." She handed the gem to Lou. "Jinx and Quackers, bring us some junk!"

Quackers flapped and Jinx skipped away.

Bong!

"I can't take these gems," Lou said. The jewels twinkled in her palm.

Trix blinked back tears and swallowed her sadness. "You turn as much junk as you can into gems, and I'll think of a spell to create your crown." Trix forced a smile onto her face. "It's no use both of us missing out."

Bong!

Lou lunged for Trix and squeezed her in the biggest hug ever. "Thanks, Trix. You really *are* my fairy godmother!"

The girls and familiars worked fast. Jinx and Quackers dropped junk at Lou's feet and she transformed every piece into another beautiful gem. The clock had nearly reached the last stroke of midnight and the other witches and familiars were disappearing one by one, their heads adorned with gleaming tiaras.

Trix grabbed Lou's witch's hat and whispered a spell. Lou's gems swirled in the air as the hat became a tiara and the jewels fell into place. Quackers flew into Lou's arms. As the clock chimed for the twelfth time,

Trix placed the tiara on Lou's head.

Lou whispered, "Thank you," as she and Quackers disappeared.

One shimmering tear fell down Trix's cheek. Jinx leaped into her arms, but not even Jinx could make Trix feel better. She looked down at her stained and ripped dress. She could fix it with a spell, but no magic was going to change the fact that it was too late.

She had failed Lulu's test.

Chapter Thirteen

Jinx's tail drooped. He felt as if he had been drenched by a rainstorm. His cat tummy felt wibbly-wobbly. He hated to see Trix cry. He had to do something to cheer her up, but it wouldn't be easy. He would have to use all his magical powers and turn up his cat charm to maximum wattage. Trix didn't know it, but she was missing her first Sisterhood of Magic Ball.

Jinx snuggled closer to Trix and purred. Oh,

how he loved his witch. He tried to make his spots sparkle – that usually made Trix happy – but he could only manage a faint twinkle.

"It's OK, Jinx," Trix said with a sniff, which told Jinx that what Trix said and what she was feeling were complete opposites.

Meow, Jinx said in his softest, sweetest voice. He was trying to tell her that it really would be OK. He added another meow to let her know how proud of her he was for helping Lou and Quackers.

Trix lowered Jinx to the floor. She wiped her eyes and straightened her dress. "We did the right thing." She sniffed and sniffed again. Her face was blotchy and her eyes red, but she smiled weakly at Jinx. "I'm really happy for Lou and Pippa," her top lip quivered, "but I'm a little sad for you and me."

Jinx began to hop and skip around Trix. If they couldn't dance at the ball, at least they could dance with each other. As if by magic, music started to play. It was dancing music, the kind that made his tail swish. The music wrapped them in a snuggly hug of sound.

"May I have this dance, Jinx Jingle Jangle?" Trix asked and curtseyed.

Jinx bowed his head and extended one front paw to accept her invitation. Trix swooped him up in her arms.

"Maybe we could take a sneaky peek at what the other witches are doing," Trix said as she swayed in time to the music and rocked Jinx back and forth.

Jinx's brain worked at double-time, thinking about the reasons that was a good idea and the reasons it was a bad one. His thoughts were like a football bouncing back and forth from goal to goal. Before he could make up his mind, Trix had already uttered a spell and they were swept away.

They were whisked right out of the cellar and twirled and swirled through Magic Mansion as if the music were leading them. They floated up, up, up a magical moving staircase. Jinx noticed that Trix's feet weren't touching the floor. She giggled and Jinx's spots sparkled as the music led them to a balcony overlooking the grand ballroom.

The ballroom was full of women and girls who

looked as if they had leaped off the pages of a fashion magazine. It was the most glamorous party in the history of glamorousness. Jinx blinked at the dazzling flashes created by the gems on the witches' silvery sashes.

An impressive voice boomed above the music and the chatter of the party. "Fairy Godmother Regina is proud to present Philippa Josephine Taylor and her familiar, Duchess Violet Von Twitch."

A spotlight focused on a beautiful blonde girl in a glistening green gown with a high ponytail and a lavender rat perched on her shoulder.

"Oh, that's Pippa and Twitch," Trix whispered in Jinx's ear. "Don't they look magical?"

Jinx nodded and nodded. The scene was like something from a fairy tale; everything was perfectly beautiful. Each witch and familiar were announced as they entered the ballroom. Jinx felt a sting of disappointment as he imagined being presented to the Sisterhood of Magic. His name would ring out and all heads would turn. His spots would sparkle, and he would bow . . . but it wasn't helpful to think about what might have been. Jinx stopped himself.

Instead, Jinx remembered the time he had sneaked Trix to Magic Mansion when she'd first learned that she was a witch. Lulu had shown them that all witches looked beautiful when they were at Magic Mansion, because witches always saw the best in people.

Jinx spotted Lou and Quackers among the magical gathering. He pointed his paw.

"Lou looks so happy," Trix said. Any hint of sadness had vanished from her voice now. Jinx could feel it too. Attending the ball would have been wonderful, but he and his witch could feel proud that they'd helped someone else.

"I wish we could go to the party," Trix said. "But I didn't finish my tiara in time. And," Trix looked down at her dress and wiggled her bare foot, "I couldn't go like this." The music swirled around Trix and Jinx.

"Maybe we could get a closer look?" Trix said and whispered another spell. Jinx wasn't sure that was a good idea.

They inched closer and closer to the railing, floating higher and higher and twirling faster and faster until the dance wasn't so much fun any more.

Jinx clung to Trix, and she held him close as her dress whipped around them.

Trix's face took on a greenish tinge. Jinx felt a bit sick, too, from all the spinning. Trix tried to start another spell. "Whirling and twirling like a spinning top." They spun faster and higher until they flew over the railing so that they were now dangling in mid-air above the ballroom.

Trix tried again. "Whirling and twirling like a spinning top." They were heading straight for the massive chandelier. "I'm feeling sick, so please make it stop!"

Jinx's head jerked back as they came to a stop only inches above the chandelier that glimmered and tinkled in the light and music of the ballroom.

"That was close," Trix said, but she spoke too soon.

Jinx suddenly felt himself falling and then they crashed into the chandelier. Trix hooked her leg around it as they tumbled upside down. Her witch's hat somersaulted to the floor. Jinx slowly slithered from Trix's grasp. He pawed and clawed at Trix's once beautiful dress until he caught hold, with a bounce, on the hem. He dug in his claws as

he and Trix swung back and forth, dangling like a
crystal from the chandelier.

"Creeping, crawling and catastrophic cats!" Trix
screamed.

Chapter Fourteen

And that's how Trix and Jinx found themselves hanging upside down from the chandelier. Trix could feel herself slipping and hear her dress ripping. The music stopped with a screech of violins as every witch in the room looked up and gasped.

Trix locked eyes with Lou, who smiled a wide smile that made Trix feel as if everything would all somehow be OK. Then Lou raised her arms over her head and shouted, "*Trix has been helpful, gracious and wise. Guide her down gently for an amazing surprise!*"

Trix held tightly to Jinx as she spun right-side up, glided to the floor and landed next to Lou. Her cheeks flushed. How embarrassing! All the witches in the Sisterhood of Magic were staring at her. She searched for Lulu or Aunt Belle. She needed to see a friendly face.

Instead, Stella stepped clear of the crowd. "You sure know how to make a fool of yourself, Trix," Stella muttered so only Trix could hear.

But Trix couldn't feel any worse than she already did. In fact, she couldn't feel lower if she sank to the cellar and then kept right on tunnelling until she reached the molten centre of the Earth.

Trix hugged Jinx more tightly and buried her face in his fur. He was so soft, and the low rumble of his purrs eased the sting of her tears. When she hugged him like that, he felt much bigger than a tiny kitten. He definitely owned a huge part of her heart. Trix reminded herself that, no matter what happened next, Jinx was her familiar and friend and nothing could take that away.

Trix felt an arm around her shoulders. She looked up to find Aunt Belle by her side.

"I'm so sorry," Trix whispered to her aunt. "I've let you down."

Aunt Belle hugged her close and wiped away Trix's tears. "No, you haven't. I'm very proud of you, Trix."

Maybe Trix's ears weren't working. She could have sworn Aunt Belle had said she was proud of her!

"I am very proud of my niece, Trixibelle Morgan, the best and brightest new witch in the Sisterhood of Magic," Aunt Belle shouted.

Had her aunt gone crazy? The crowd circled around Trix, Aunt Belle and Lou. Trix tried to think of an invisibility spell. Why was her aunt drawing attention to the fact that Trix had completely and utterly failed her test?

"I've got a little surprise for you," Lou said.

"When is the test not the test?" Aunt Belle asked. "And a puzzle only one piece of a bigger puzzle?"

Trix's heart sank. Another riddle!

The fairy godmothers joined hands and the room erupted in a shower of confetti that swept around Lou. Trix rubbed her eyes. She could no longer see Lou in the tornado of shimmering light.

"What's happening?" Trix asked everyone and no one.

"You'll see," Aunt Belle said, hugging Trix and Jinx a tiny bit tighter.

"Ta-da!" everyone shouted as the air cleared.

Lou wasn't Lou any more.

Lou had transformed into . . .

"Lulu?" Trix breathed.

Chapter Fifteen

Lulu twirled in her glimmering lacy black gown and her dazzling bangles jingle-jangled.

"I'm sorry I had to trick blue, true, YOU," Lulu told Trix with a wink.

And, wow, had Trix been fooled! Lulu was a good actress as well as a spectacular witch, but Trix didn't understand why Lulu had been in disguise.

"Congratulations to one and all!" Lulu said. "You were magically marvellous. Every witch has passed her test with a rainbow of flying colours. We have an exceptional class of witches this year!"

Trix tapped Lulu's arm. "Even me?"

"*Especially* you!" Lulu exclaimed. "Each witch was offered the chance to help another witch, and *almost* every witch-in-training helped another girl in need. But Trix went above and beyond everyone else. She sacrificed her chance to finish the test so that another witch could succeed. Trix acted with the instincts of a true fairy godmother and, because of that, she has earned an extra-special reward."

Trix felt a rush of pride. She'd done that?

The fairy godmothers lined up in front of Trix. Jinx hopped down and scampered away. Where was he going now? Trix felt a bit lost, being the centre of attention without him by her side. She realised again how terrible she must look. Her hair was a mess. Her dress was stained and ripped. She only had one shoe.

One by one the fairy godmothers bowed to Trix and then, with a wave of their magical wands, they each gave Trix a gift. One changed her tattered gown from sunny yellow to shimmering snow-white. Another fairy godmother cast a spell to smooth and curl Trix's hair so that it bounced at her shoulders. Some gave her jewellery, others added jewels to her gown. Lulu and Aunt Belle were the last in line.

"It is our job to crown you," Aunt Belle explained, painting the air above Trix's head with her magic wand.

"You're the belle of the ball," Lulu and Aunt Belle announced in unison. With a flick of their wrists and a double click of their fingers, the most amazing, sparkling tiara appeared above Trix and slowly lowered onto her head.

"It's beautiful," Trix sighed as she caught sight of her reflection in the mirrored walls of the grand ballroom. She looked like a magical princess.

Everything was perfect except for one

teeny-tiny detail. Trix tucked her bare foot under the hem of her gown. Then she smiled. If only having one shoe was good enough for Cinderella, it was good enough for her!

Just then Jinx came racing in. He was slipping and sliding across the dance floor. He had something in his mouth. As he dropped it at her feet, Trix realised what it was.

"My missing shoe!" she exclaimed. "Thanks, Jinx!"

Trix slipped on her shoe as the orchestra began to play again. The music set her toes tapping. Aunt Belle grabbed one hand and Lulu the other.

Pippa, Becka and Cara danced over to them. "Congratulations!" they said to Trix.

"Well done," Stella said as she joined in. "I knew you would do it."

"Stella, you could learn a thing or two from Trix," Lulu told her. "I'm afraid that you will lose a gem because of your dirty tricks tonight." Lulu pointed to the blue gem on Stella's sash and it vanished with a *poof*! "You are a superior witch, Stella, but sometimes an unkind person. If you want to be a fairy godmother one day, you need to polish up your niceness and think of others first."

Stella nodded. "I will try." She looked sad.

"But tonight," Lulu hugged Stella, "we celebrate the best in everyone!"

Lulu, Aunt Belle and all of Trix's friends clasped hands and danced in a big circle. Their familiars flew or scampered into the centre and danced around too.

This was a truly magical moment. The grand ballroom glowed with the magic of friendship and fun! Trix felt sparklier than the most sparkly diamond and happier than the happiest clown. This was a moment she would remember for ever. It was the first moment she really and truly believed that she could be a fairy godmother one day.